First published 2000 by Walker Books Ltd
87 Vauxhall Walk, London SE11 5HJ

2 4 6 8 10 9 7 5 3 1

Based on the Audio Visual series "Maisy" A King Rollo Films Production for
Universal Pictures Visual Programming. Original script by Andrew Brenner

This book has been typeset in Lucy Cousins Typeface

Printed in Hong Kong

British Library Cataloguing in Publication Data
A catalogue record for this book is
available from the British Library

0-7445-7514-7 (hb)
0-7445-7578-9 (pb)

Maisy's Bus

Lucy Cousins

WALKER BOOKS

AND SUBSIDIARIES

LONDON • BOSTON • SYDNEY

Maisy is driving her bus today.

Who will be at bus stop number 1?

It's Cyril.

Hello, Cyril.

Little Black Cat
is waiting at bus
stop number 2.

Hello,
Little Black Cat.

Brmm, brmm!

Who will be at bus stop number 3?

It's Tallulah,
waiting in the rain.

Hello, Tallulah.

Eddie is waiting at bus stop number 4.

Will there be room on the bus?

Hooray! There's room for everyone.

Brmm, brmm! Where is Maisy going now?

Bus stop number 5.

It's time to get off, everyone.

Oops! Wake up,
Little Black Cat.

This is the last stop.

Bye bye, everyone.
Bye bye, Maisy.

Brmm, brmm!